Mary Jane —
Warmest regards,

It Doesn't Have to be pink

By Janelle A. Baliko

Illustrated by Bethany Hackmann

Mercury Publishing Services

who worked with and guided me

to self-publishing

©2007 by Janelle A. Baliko
Printed in Hong Kong.
ISBN-13: 978-0-9799012-0-1
ISBN-10: 0-9799012-0-0

Hi, I am Sofia.

Today, I am going to take you on an adventure through my life where I will make many decisions – the types of decisions that girls everywhere face every day. I love being a girl and playing girl games and dressing in pink. But some days, I may choose to wear blue instead of pink or to play with my brother instead of with other little girls. I know that it is okay to make these decisions because they make me happy. I also know that even if I don't wear pink, I am still a little girl.

Today I am wearing a pink sundress with my
long, curly, blond hair pulled back
into a ponytail to keep it out of my eyes.

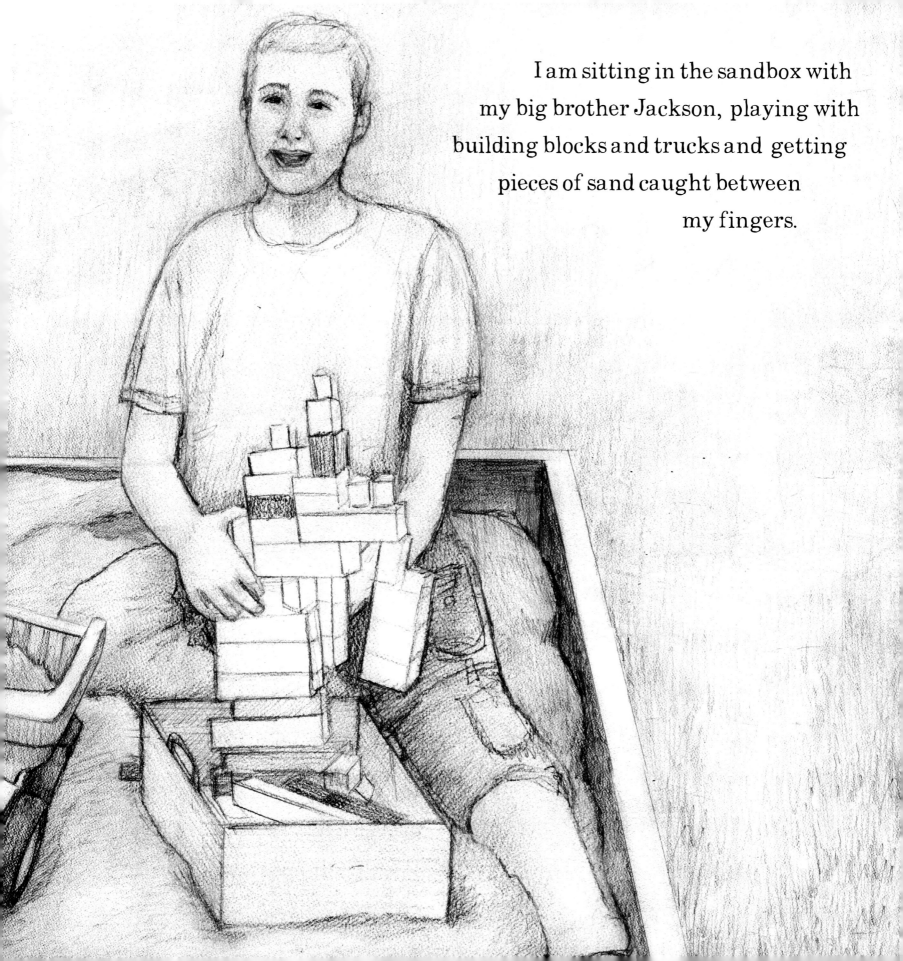

I am sitting in the sandbox with
my big brother Jackson, playing with
building blocks and trucks and getting
pieces of sand caught between
my fingers.

Jackson encourages me to build the tallest of buildings to match the one he's just built with multi-colored blocks. Sure enough, I match my brother's building, floor-by-floor and color-by-color.

Jackson smiles at me and tells me that I could be an architect some day.

He explains to me that as an architect, I will be able to design and create real buildings when I get older.

I fall asleep that night dreaming of such a possibility.

Today I am at school and my friends are jumping rope on the playground during recess when I notice a slow-crawling fuzzy black caterpillar on the sidewalk.

My friends call out for me to stay and play with them instead of chasing bugs, but I decide to follow the caterpillar.

I save the caterpillar from bicycles
by picking it up off the sidewalk and placing it
in the grass.

I don't mind that my hands get a little dirty
while caring for the caterpillar.

I go home from school a happy girl
and ask my mommy if it is okay for me
to save bugs instead of jumping rope
with my friends.

I tell her that what I did for the soft little
caterpillar makes me very happy inside.

My mommy tells me
that saving the
caterpillar is a very good
deed. She says that it
doesn't matter that I am
a girl –

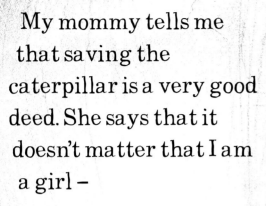

I should do
whatever I feel is
right in my heart.

My mommy hugs
me and tells me
that because of
my love of life,
even for a tiny
caterpillar,

I might one day become a biologist.

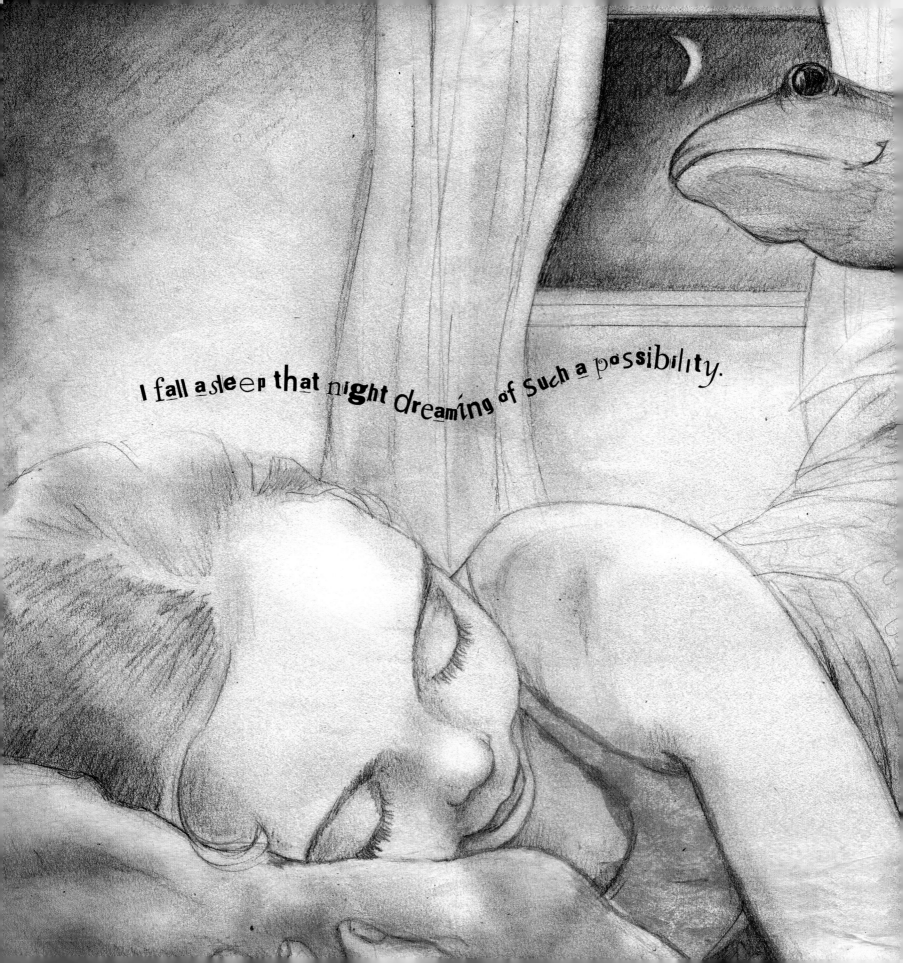

I fall asleep that night dreaming of such a possibility.

Today our local community center is holding an event where kids can sign up for the sports they want to join. My friends and I are meeting there so we can sign up for different activities.

Walking into the center, I join my group of friends who are
signing up to be cheerleaders, so I am starting to feel a bit
pressured to be a cheerleader, too.

I love to dance and was even in a gymnastics class when I was younger, but I don't feel like cheerleading is what I want to do right now.

My friends tell me that we should all stick together and join the cheerleading team.

After thinking long and hard, I stand up from my seat and quietly walk over to the cheerleading sign-up table.

I stop, look back at my friends, slowly move to the next table and confidently sign up for the soccer team.

Two of my friends quickly join my side and sign up to play soccer too.

Our other friends are disappointed, but they hug us anyway because they know we selected the best activity for ourselves.

I go home from
school that day
excited as ever
about my future as a
soccer player.

When I explain my
decision to my daddy,
he hugs me tightly. He
explains how proud
he is that I made my
own decision despite
the pressure of my
friends.

He smiles and tells me
that this could be the
beginning of my life
as a professional
athlete.

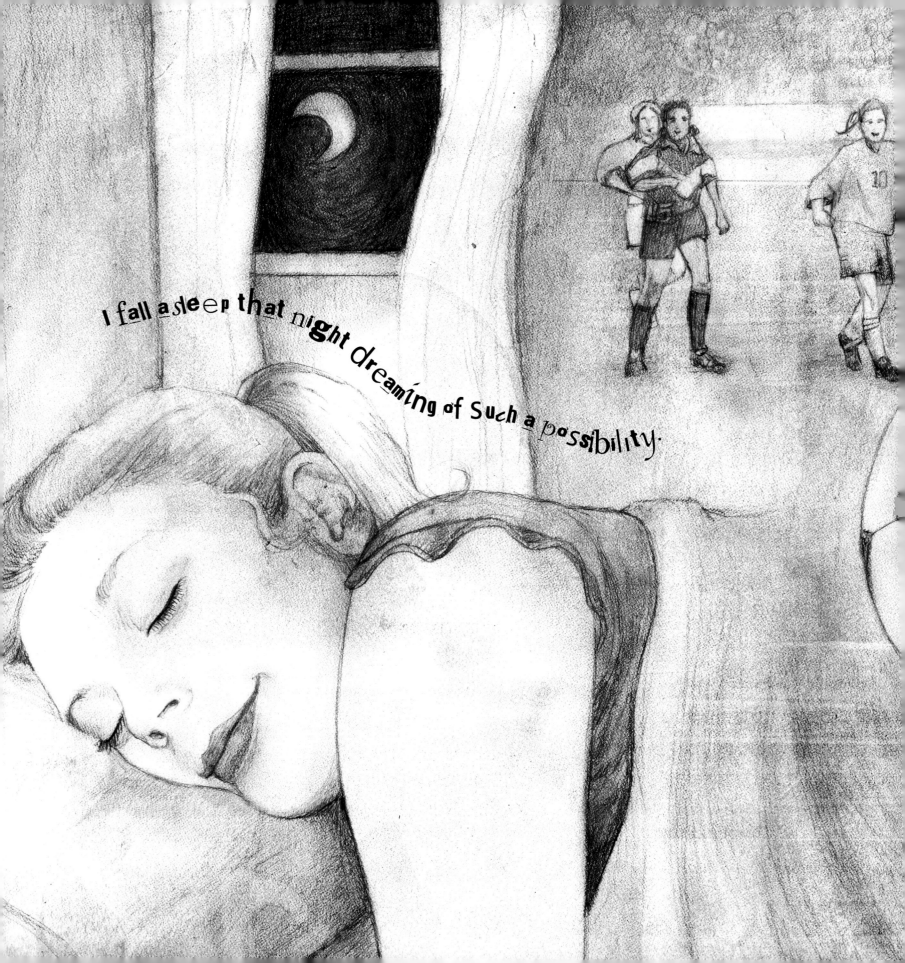

I fall asleep that night dreaming of such a possibility.

I hope you have enjoyed this small
part of my journey as a young girl.

As I say good-bye, I hope you
understand that you will always have the
opportunity to express yourself as a girl.
Being a girl is special and amazing and full
of choices. And as you journey through your
own life, you will choose your favorite colors,
activities, sports and many, many other things.
You should make choices that make you happy.

You can even choose a new favorite
color every day, and it doesn't
always have to be **pink**.

Thank-you

A tremendous thank you to Bethany Hackmann who made my words dance through her phenomenal illustrations; this book would not be what it is without her extraordinary talent

A special thanks to my family: Mom, Dad, Chris and Allison, Eric and Heidi, Ryan, Memere and Anne for their undying love and support throughout life's obstacles and achievements, this book for one, and for always believing in me, pushing me to my true potential and encouraging me to not always wear pink.

To the fabulous innocence of Jacob, Mase and Maddie

To Cara Valentino, my partner-in-crime who enthusiastically helped edit this book and focus it in the right direction

To Sibby and Clay for being two of my biggest cheerleaders

To my business partners, Tracey Williams and Wendy McAllister for supporting this book while establishing and building our company, in addition to running each of our own separate businesses

To Douglas A. Grimm who positively influenced the writing of this book by providing me the mental opportunity and capacity for reaching this achievement at this moment in my life

To the strong women who have served as my mentors over the years: Wendy Cramer, Nadine Genet, Deborah Chiao, Jean Lenderman, Linda Matesevac – I would not be at this point in my life without your encouragement, expertise, patience and support of my education and career path

To Rich at Heck Yeah! Studio, Inc. for his artistic ability to create the best website ever: www.itdoesnthavetobepink.com

To my friends at Mercury Publishing Services for their friendship and professional guidance allowing me to self-publish this book

To those who do everything in their power to keep me healthy: Dawit Assefa, Dr. Sheila Levin, Marie Parlatto, Dr. Paula Radecki, Dr. William Condrell, Dr. Alison Ehrlich

A very special thank you to Dr. Alan Lake, Dr. Faith Hackett and Dr. Marjorie Kanof for taking such special care of me as a young patient – you paved the way for me to lead and know a healthy and 'normal' life

To everyone who has touched my life in a positive way through its many obstacles. To all of my family and friends who encourage me to participate in the most fun life-style ever, you are so important and special to me beyond words

Oma, Opa, Pepere, and Tyree, you are always with me

Janelle Baliko

Bethany Hackmann

A native of Southern Maryland and graduate of York College of PA, Janelle currently resides in Alexandria, VA as the owner of a marketing consulting company and a managing partner in a secondary consulting firm. She enjoys seeking and accepting new challenges and volunteering for the community. She is expecting her second book, *It Doesn't Have to be Green*, to be available in summer 2008. For more information about *It Doesn't Have to be Pink* and Janelle's interests, please visit www.itdoesnthavetobepink.com.

is living out her childhood dreams as a graphic designer, painter, and illustrator. She has recently moved to Decorah, IA; closer to family members who love stories even more than she does.